Tales of Familiars:

The First Mortal Realm Witch Series Companion

Jennifer Priester

Tales of Familiars:
The First Mortal Realm Witch Series Companion
By Jennifer Priester

Copyright © 2014 by Jennifer Priester

Publisher: A & M Moonlight Creations
www.mortalrealmwitch.com, and
A & M Moonlight Creations on Facebook

Art work and layout by Jennifer Priester
Artistic support by Vicky Mehls
Book management by Janet Bennett

ISBN: 978-1-938783-02-9

Printed in the United States of America

Contents

Magical Teachings from Familiars

Time's Up?

Introduction

Welcome to the first Mortal Realm Witch Series companion book *Tales of Familiars*!

Animals often make good teachers. No one knows this better than witches and warlocks. In this first Series companion book you will read ten different stories, each of which is told by a familiar and will help you understand the important role these special animals play in teaching witches and warlocks.

Be sure to look for the first three books in the Mortal Realm Witch Series, which are available now, to enjoy even more adventures with familiars, witches and warlocks, *Mortal Realm Witch: Learning About Magic, Mortal Realm Witch: The Magic Continues,* and *Mortal Realm Witch: Realms Unite?*

And keep watch for additional books in the Series coming soon.

To learn about the Series and discover more magic, visit our website at **www.mortalrealmwitch.com.**

And now let the magic begin!

Prologue

The average image that most mortals have of a witch is probably someone dressed completely in black. They have a pointy hat, a large pointed nose, a couple warts, a broomstick, a black cat and they use black magic. Most witches do not look like that, although there are a few.

The world as you know it is called the Mortal Realm. It is called this because mortals are in charge of it.

The other realm that exists is actually called that—it is known by most witches as the Other Realm. The Other Realm is the realm where witches, warlocks, and familiars live. Warlocks are male witches and familiars are talking animals who teach a witch or warlock their magic.

Most mortals don't know about the Other Realm and can't visit or live there. But witches, warlocks, and familiars know about and sometimes visit and live in the Mortal Realm.

The word "witches" happens to be the term used when talking about witches, warlocks, and familiars as a group.

You already know that witches use magic. Magic is the ability to make things happen by simply thinking about what you want, and then pointing, waving your hands, or saying a quick spell.

Most of the time saying a spell is a lot like reciting a short poem in which the last word of each line must rhyme. Actually, they don't have to rhyme, but for the spell to be most effective it really should. An example of an effective spell would be:

I am feeling a little bored today
Give me the wings of a dragon so I can fly
up, up, and away.

Having magic also gives a witch the ability to create magical potions.

Magical potions can be made up of charmed ingredients, found only in the Other Realm, or they can include regular Mortal Realm ingredients found in both Realms.

Witches usually use recipes to create magic potions. A recipe for a magical potion might look something like this:

1 cup Unicorn horn
(unicorns naturally shed their horns
during winter just like deer)
2 cloves of garlic
2 tsp. vinegar
3 cups sugar
4 oz. pond water
Stir ingredients together in a
small pot or cauldron
and boil for 10 - 15 minutes.

This is actually the recipe used to create an Angel Frog. This is a type of frog that can be used against enemies. The frog is pure white and it has the power to enter anyone's mind. Unfortunately, it is limited to only being able to go into someone's mind when they are asleep, so unless your enemy is dreaming about you it is useless.

Now, when doing a potion you must follow the instructions exactly. For example, if you decided not to use sugar your results would be very different.

Instead of creating the Angel Frog you would now have created a Demon Frog which can be red, black, orange or any mixture of these colors.

The Demon Frog can enter into anyone's mind at any time and it can even search for hidden thoughts. This makes it very effective to find out if an enemy is planning something against you.

Unfortunately, many witches and mortals would believe that by creating this creature a witch is using black magic, but black magic isn't actually a type of magic that exists.

There are two types of magic in existence. I'm sure you know of the one type, witchcraft.

Witchcraft is the type of magic that witches and warlocks use. Familiars can't do magic of any kind.

Witches are born with witchcraft. At first a witch usually believes that witchcraft has infinite possibilities, but it really doesn't. But it takes a long time to learn witchcraft, and a lot of practice to get really good at it.

The other type of magic is known as natural magic. Witches can't use this type of magic, but mortals can. Natural magic comes from nature and only exists in the Mortal Realm.

It can be harnessed and controlled by mortals, and this type of magic doesn't have any limitations.

So welcome a new world of magic! The stories you are about to read will help you learn even more about the magic in both Realms. Enjoy!

Magical Teachings

From Familiars

Magical Teachings from Familiars

Prelude: Part One

You may already know that a familiar is a talking animal who teaches magic to a witch or warlock. What you may not know is in order to be a familiar you don't need to have been a witch or a warlock first.

Actually, in the past familiars were talking animals that had never been human. Other Realm animals already know everything that they need to except for how to be a familiar. Familiars lived in the Other Realm and learned magic alongside their owners.

They couldn't do any magic, but it was discovered that they could remember what they learned better than the humans. This made them good assistants and later, good teachers.

It wasn't long before the Witches Council decided that if the owners of familiars learned magic better than those without them, then the ones who needed extra help with their magic would learn better by becoming familiars themselves.

While being a familiar helped them in some areas, the Witches Council had forgotten that familiars had no ability to actually do magic.

Then the Council got a better idea. They decided that all witches would be required to have a familiar.

This worked well, but then the Witches Council had yet another problem to work out.

It turned out that the witches were better at magic, but many started to use it in ways that were against the rules. The standard punishment at the time had been to take away their powers and sentence them to spend time in the Mortal Realm.

It wasn't the best way to do things, however. It seemed that once they got their powers back, most hadn't learned anything from it, and they went right back to using their powers however they wanted.

After some thought about this problem, the Witches Council decided to try something new. The goal was for the witch or warlock to be punished and learn something from it.

So a new system was set up, and it worked so well that it is the one that is still used today. In case you aren't sure about how the system works, I will explain it.

First, a witch or warlock gets into trouble.

Second the punishment is decided. The Head of the Witches Council decides whether to suspend their powers, turn them into a familiar, or have them lose their powers forever. This is when they become a mortal and live in the Mortal Realm forever.

Third, the Head of the Witches Council decides on an animal that fits the punishment.

Fourth, they are turned into the animal and the length of time of the sentence is decided.

Fifth, they are then assigned to a witch or warlock to train until their sentence is up.

That is how the system works.

The following stories show how some familiars deal with their situations, and what they and their witch or warlock learn from them.

Picture Perfect

Picture Perfect

I am a badger. My name is Scout and I have been a familiar my whole life. I am currently working with a warlock by the name of Falcon.

Since I have never been a warlock myself, I don't know everything about magic. But I have gone through familiar training and have read the Other Realm rulebook for familiars.

I also constantly review the spell books. I like to work with Falcon on spells that not only teach him magic but other lessons as well. The story I am about to tell you happens to be about one of these times.

"That is a cool, yet useless spell!" Falcon said.

"Not completely useless," I replied.

"Well it definitely didn't do what I wanted it to," Falcon exclaimed.

"That's because the spell that you want to use doesn't exist," I explained patiently.

If you are confused right now,
it won't last long because here is what
happened.

Falcon has always liked paintings.
Both of his parents are artists. Falcon
himself doesn't paint pictures, but he loves
to look at them.

It was during one of these times
when Falcon tried out a new spell.

He was looking at a painting that
his mom had done of a park. In the
picture the sun was shining, and the sky
was blue with only a few clouds. There
was also a boy and his dad playing catch.
A family of two girls, a mother, a father,
and a cat were having a picnic. There was
also a woman walking a Beagle, and a
man playing fetch with a Toy Fox Terrier.

To Falcon the painting looked
perfect.

"Why can't my life be perfect like a
painting?" Falcon asked out loud.

"Well, your life could be picture
perfect," I replied. "You could actually live
inside a painting."

"How?" Falcon asked curiously.

"You could use a spell called Picture Perfect," I explained.

Falcon then went to find his spell book. As soon as he found the right spell he performed it. Instantly Falcon and I became a part of his mom's painting.

At first Falcon liked it, but he soon realized that he couldn't live in a painting forever.

"This is boring," Falcon complained.

"What did you expect? We are in a painting," I replied.

"I thought that once we entered the painting it would come to life," Falcon said.

"Sorry, but the spell doesn't work that way. What you see from the outside of a painting, you get from the inside as well."

"So you mean that nothing will ever move or change?" he asked.

"Exactly," I said.

Falcon then undid the spell and this is where you came in earlier. Falcon was just saying how the spell was useless, but it wasn't. I wanted him to see that picture perfect is really just a term, not a reality.

I told Falcon that the spell he wanted didn't exist. Falcon then asked me, "Then how do I get the perfect life?"

"By working hard. You know, the mortal way," I replied. Then I added, "Even if you get what you think you want, it still may not be perfect."

"But couldn't I use magic to find out?" Falcon asked.

"Only if you want to end up a familiar like me," I warned him.

"Oh, that's not really my idea of a perfect life," Falcon said.

"I didn't think that it was, although it works fine for me," I said.

"Only because you have always been a familiar," Falcon said.

"That's probably true. By the way, what is your idea of a perfect life?" I asked.

"I don't know, but I like dreaming about it."

"Maybe you could paint what you dream about. Then for a short time, as you paint it and then later when you look at it, you can live your perfect life," I suggested.

"What do you mean?" Falcon asked.

"When you dream, does it ever feel real to you?" I asked.

"Almost all the time, why?" he asked.

"Well then for now you can live anything that you want through dreaming, and extend the fun of dreaming by painting your ideas of perfection until maybe one day you know exactly what you want and live it for real," I suggested.

"That does sound like fun. I'll start now," said Falcon excitedly.

"What are you going to paint first?"

"You!" Falcon exclaimed.

"Why is that?" I asked him.

"Because you are my idea of a perfect familiar," Falcon said.

Falcon then went into the garage where all the art stuff was located. I followed him. As soon as he had everything he needed, Falcon started painting.

When the painting was done he showed it to me. It looked a little bit like me. I tried to tell him exactly what I thought about it without sounding as if I didn't like it, but Falcon figured it out anyway.

It didn't bother Falcon that his first painting wasn't very good. He said that doing it was fun, and he knows that he will improve over time so he is definitely going to continue painting and dreaming about his picture perfect life.

A
Powerful
Friendship

A Powerful Friendship

My name is Mieko and I am a squirrel. Once I was a witch. I lived in the Mortal Realm and had a job that involved illegally cutting down trees.

I wanted the money, but didn't want to do the work for it so I used magic to cut them down.

It wasn't long until DWW caught me and sentenced me to fifty years as a squirrel. You might wonder why she chose a squirrel.

DWW thought that besides being punished for my irresponsible use of magic, I should also learn to be more respectful of trees. So now instead of cutting them down, I am living in one.

The worst part about my punishment is that my witch lives right near the area where I used to work. My witch's name is Ashta.

"I am so glad that's over," Ashta said.

"Yeah, me too," I replied.

I was sitting in a tree with Ashta who was on a branch directly below me. I guess you are wondering what we were talking about. Well, I'll tell you. It all began with a necklace.

About one month ago, Ashta got a friendship necklace from her best friend, Jessica.

"Mieko, look what I got," Ashta said.

"A necklace, how nice. Where did you get it?" I asked, not really caring or bothering to really look at it.

"Jessica gave it to me," she explained.

"Okay," I said, still not really paying much attention.

For the next few weeks, every time Ashta wore the necklace she had lots of good luck, and whenever she thought about her friend, Jessica would show up soon after.

At the time, I didn't think much about it because Ashta and Jessica are together a lot, but after a while they started fighting.

One day after coming home from school and fighting with Jessica, Ashta said that the more they fought the more the necklace burned.

At first I thought that she was imagining it, but then I noticed that the necklace was glowing.

"Ashta, can I see your necklace for a minute?" I asked.

"Sure," she said.

As soon as she took it off and put it down in front of me, it stopped glowing.

I looked at it for a minute and realized that I had seen this necklace before at a cheap shop in the Other Realm back when I was a witch. DWW had shut the shop down for selling things with messed up magical symbols on them.

The necklace Ashta had gotten from Jessica was circular and had an M on the top with a crooked B which was partially attached to the left side of the M. Next to the B was a normal looking F which was partially attached to the other side of the M. The letters were bubble like letters, but it was inside and around the letters that were the magical symbols.

"It's a magical necklace," I said.

"How can you tell?" Ashta asked.

"It has magical symbols on it," I explained.

"M, B, and F are symbols?" Ashta asked.

"No, look at the gray areas," I said. The necklace was gray with black letters.

"Those are the symbols?"

"Yes."

"What do they mean?" she asked.

"Well, the crescent shaped one on the left side by the M and B means good luck. This would explain why you were having good luck whenever you wore it," I explained.

"The upside down triangle above the M and the symbol in the middle of the necklace are actually supposed to be connected. If connected it would mean trust, but apart it means the exact opposite. This is the reason the necklace burns every time you and Jessica fight," I continued.

"Wow," exclaimed Ashta. "OK, go on, what else do you see?"

"The two dots in the B mean magnetic, which is why every time you thought about Jessica she would soon appear," I said.

"The big symbol on the right side after the F means friendship. If you removed the symbol from the necklace, it would look like clay that had an F shoved into the side and then removed. Normally this symbol would bring you closer to your friend, but the last symbol, the small one between the bottom of the B and F, means broken," I explained.

"So, basically what is happening is that as long as you trust Jessica, whenever you wear the necklace you will have good luck and be able to see her whenever you want. The broken sign and the messed up trust sign aren't as powerful as the friendship sign at first, but the more you fight with Jessica the more trust you lose, and the more trust you lose the more the necklace will burn. You also will have lots of bad luck when you wear it," I concluded.

"So, what do I do?" Ashta asked.

"You need to stop wearing the necklace for a while and fix your friendship."

"But she will be madder at me if I don't wear it!" Ashta exclaimed.

"If you do wear it and you two get into a big enough fight, the necklace could get really powerful. This means that even if you aren't wearing it, the necklace will still be able to affect you," I warned her.

"All right, I won't wear it," Ashta said.

The next day she did wear it even though she said that she wouldn't. She and Jessica ended up in a big fight and Ashta said that the necklace was now almost too hot to hold.

"I told you not to wear it," I said.

"I know, but I had to!" she said.

"Well, now the only thing you can do is get rid of it," I explained.

"You mean put it away somewhere?" she asked.

"No, I mean destroy it," I said. "That is the only solution."

"All right, but once I do, can I keep what's left?"

"I guess, *if* there is anything left."

Ashta then went into the house where I am not allowed. In Ashta's window I saw a bright flash of light and soon after she came out carrying a small box and a shovel. She then buried the box under our tree.

"Now, hopefully it has lost all of its power," I said.

"You mean it might not? Ashta asked.

"It's hard to tell with magical things. Some powers can be removed if the object is destroyed and others have to be removed by the person who created it," I explained.

That night Ashta called Jessica and they still fought. Ashta said that she could still feel the necklace's power, so I told her to find out where Jessica had gotten it.

The next day was Saturday. As soon as Ashta found out where Jessica had gotten the necklace, we went to the shop. It was located just a few blocks away from Ashta's house.

As soon as we walked into the shop, I recognized the warlock in charge of it.

"If you destroyed it, then its powers should be gone," he said.

"Ashta, are you sure you destroyed it?" I asked.

"No, I didn't. I just zapped myself a box and shovel and put it into the box. The bright light you saw was just an illusion to make you think I had destroyed it," she confessed.

"Well, then destroy it and your problems are over," the warlock said.

Back at home, Ashta and I dug up the necklace. Ashta opened the box and picked up the necklace, but it was too hot for her to hold.

This time I watched as Ashta's magic destroyed it. The necklace came apart and each symbol and letter stood apart from each other. Ashta then reburied it.

That night, Ashta called Jessica and tried to make up with her, but something made them fight instead.

I was sitting on the windowsill watching her at the time, and noticed that Ashta's hand was glowing slightly. I looked closer and recognized the symbols from the necklace.

The next chance I got I asked her, "Did you get burned by the necklace?"

"Yeah, why?" she asked.

"Because it burned the symbols into your hand," I said.

"It did?" she asked looking closely at her hand.

"Yes, it did, and tomorrow we are going back to the shop to see if that warlock knows how to fix this."

"Okay," she said. "I hope we can get this fixed and soon."

When we arrived at the shop the next day, the first thing I noticed was an out of business sign on the window.

"He's gone!" I said.

"Now what?" Ashta asked.

"I guess now we have to go see DWW," I suggested. "She's the only one who will know what to do."

"All right," agreed Ashta.

We then went home, unburied the necklace, and then Ashta zapped us into the Other Realm.

After explaining our problem to DWW, she asked if she could see the necklace. Ashta gave her the box with the pieces in it.

DWW took out the pieces and put the necklace back together the way it was supposed to be. She removed the broken symbol and connected the two pieces of the trust symbol.

She then told Ashta to hold the necklace the way she did when it burned her and concentrate on heating it up.

DWW explained that by burning the new symbol onto the old one that the symbols would cancel each other out.

As soon as Ashta did this, DWW said that she could keep the necklace because it would now be like wearing a normal necklace.

Within the next week, Ashta and Jessica's relationship returned to normal, and Jessica never noticed the difference in the necklace.

But that wasn't all that happened that week.

Later that week, DWW also caught the warlock in charge of the shop. He is now going to be spending several hundred years as a ferret.

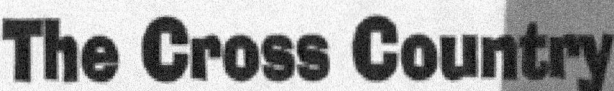

The Cross Country

Frog Race

The Cross Country Frog Race

My name is Marco and I am a Red Eyed Tree Frog. DWW turned me into one for twenty-five years.

Twenty-five years is the shortest amount of time that a witch or warlock can be sentenced. I wouldn't have had to spend any time at all as a frog if frogs could keep quiet.

I gave all frogs in the Mortal Realm the ability to talk, which I didn't see as a problem until mortals heard them talking.

After that I got called into the Other Realm to see DWW. She said that if I wanted to talk to frogs, then for the next twenty-five years I would get to be one. She then assigned me to a warlock named Billy.

"So you admit that it is harder to get used to being a frog than you thought," I said.

"Yeah, I guess," Billy replied.

You can probably tell from this short conversation that Billy had also been a frog for a little while.

You probably don't know how this happened. Well, since you don't know I will tell you. This all started with a race...a frog race.

Billy brought his friends home from school one day and they all brought wild frogs that they had caught with them.

At first I thought that Billy wanted me to have other frogs to play with, but that wasn't his idea. Billy wanted me to race against the wild frogs that his friends had caught.

Before I say anything else about the race, you should know that Billy has three friends, all of which brought frogs.

One of Billy's friends not only brought a frog, he also brought a large cardboard box which he set down on the floor. We were in Billy's bedroom. The box had three pieces of cardboard taped inside of it which were supposed to be jumps.

Billy then grabbed me and put me in the box at one end, but he still held me down so I couldn't go anywhere.

His friends did the same thing with their frogs.

Billy then told his friends to release their frogs, which they did. After that Billy released me and told me to win this race.

At first no frogs moved; they didn't understand what they were being expected to do.

Since I knew exactly what to do, I started moving. But just as I got to the first jump, the other frogs suddenly got the idea and started to catch up to me.

I tried my hardest to stay ahead of them, but in the end all of the other frogs passed me, and I ended up losing the race.

After the race was over, Billy's friends took their frogs out of the box. When Billy took me out of the box, I could tell that he was mad.

That night Billy yelled at me for losing the race.

"You should have won!" Billy said.

"How could you expect that!" I said.

"Because you aren't really a frog so you are smarter than my friends' frogs!"

"Being smarter than them has nothing to do with racing; racing is about speed!"

"You still should have won," Billy exclaimed.

"Well, sorry if I haven't gotten used to being a frog yet!" I said defensively.

"How hard can it be?" Billy asked.

"It's hard to get used to being something that you have never been before," I explained.

"Maybe for the first few hours, but by now you should be used to it," Billy argued.

"I've only been a frog for one week. Your friends' frogs have been frogs their whole lives!" I said defensively.

"Yeah, well I bet that I could get used to being a frog in one hour and beat you in a race!" Billy bragged.

"Fine, then tomorrow we will race. You can even set up the race course any way that you want. We will have a cross country frog race," I challenged him.

"Okay!" Billy agreed.

The next day Billy set up a small course through the woodlands near his house. It went through some trees with some tree roots, sticks, and some garbage that people threw on the ground.

All these obstacles would serve as jumps. Billy planned on going back after the race and picking up the garbage.

The total number of jumps in the race was going to be ten. There was also a small pond to cross. The course started at the end of the woods and ended on the other side of the small pond.

Before the race, Billy took me behind a tree near the start of the course and set me down. He then turned himself into a frog, the same kind as I was, and we jumped to the start.

As soon as Billy said go I was ready.

I hopped through the trees to the first jump. The first jump was a small stick that was just high enough to make me have to jump over it.

I then headed toward the next jump which was a tree root that was going to be hard to clear. I jumped over it, then looked back to see Billy in the process of jumping over the small stick. So far I was going faster than he was.

Next I hopped to jump number three, a paper towel roll which was located directly off a turn in the course. I would have to be ready to jump before I could see it.

After that jump, I could tell that I was far enough ahead of Billy that I could slow down if I wanted, but I didn't want to. This *was* a competition after all.

Instead I headed to a cup, jump number four. As I came up to it, the cup started to float, which hadn't happened when Billy had shown the coarse to me earlier.

I realized that he was using his magic to try to win the race. Instead of stopping and yelling at Billy like some familiars would do, I decided to ignore it.

I then jumped as high as I could, which was twice as high as the cup was, and cleared it easily. But as I jumped it, I noticed that the cup was moving higher and higher. After I landed, I looked back and saw that it had dropped back down to the ground.

Next I headed to a bush which I had to go into and jump in three different spots to get through it. As I went through the bush, parts of it seemed to reach out and hit me on its own, but I knew that Billy was doing it. I ignored this and didn't let it slow me down.

I then headed toward the next jump, a cat's tail. The cat was sitting, and watching me approach. Its tail was slightly moving back and forth. I knew that Billy had frozen the cat, except for its tail, so I wasn't afraid as I moved towards it.

But as I jumped the tail, the cat moved. It hissed and tried to pounce on me. It missed, but I had run into its yard which was off of the course.

I turned around to look at the cat and noticed that it was now completely still, and Billy was jumping its tail.

I knew I couldn't let Billy win, but as I watched him pull further ahead, I wasn't sure that I could beat him.

I hoped that Billy had kept the cat frozen this time and I ran passed it. The cat didn't move.

I then headed toward the next jump, which Billy was also getting close to. I moved as fast as I could, but I was still behind as I jumped another tree root.

All I could do now was hope that

Billy didn't get to the last jump before I did. The last jump was a group of small rocks that were lined up in the middle of the pond.

I got to the pond and saw Billy was only halfway to the jump. I knew I could beat him now because I was catching up fast. I got to the rocks and jumped to the other side just as Billy started jumping them.

I then swam as fast as I could to get to the other end of the pond, but I got hit by a large wave just before reaching the end. I got pushed back to the rock, but it didn't matter because Billy had gotten hit with his own wave and was back at the start of the pond.

I then swam back to the end and won the race.

Back at home, Billy changed back into a human and said, "You only won because you have been a frog longer than me."

"That's exactly what I was telling

you about me and your friends' frogs," I told him.

"Oh, yeah. Well I guess that you were right," Billy replied. It was then that I knew Billy was never going to be mad at me for losing a race against real frogs again.

The Hot Party

The Hot Party

My name is JR. I am a brown, black and white English Springer Spaniel.

I got turned into one by DWW for a few hundred years after I opened a potion store in the Mortal Realm, and tried to sell magical potions.

Currently I have a warlock named Ben.

"Magic didn't make things easier this time did it?" Ben asked.

"No it didn't," I replied.

Ben and I were talking about a birthday party he threw for his friend, Jasper.

It was a Saturday afternoon. Ben and I were waiting for Jasper to arrive. The ten other people Ben and Jasper invited had already arrived. Once Jasper finally arrived, the party began.

A couple of hours later, Ben went into the house to get Jasper's cake.

While no one was looking, Ben pointed at the candles getting ready to magically light them. Just as he was getting ready to fire, Jasper came up behind him and said, "Man, this is one hot party!"

Ben quickly lowered his finger, but it was too late to stop the magic. Instead of lighting the candles, he set the rug on fire.

"This party is hot in more ways than one," I whispered to Ben.

"What do you mean?" he whispered back.

"Look down."

Ben looked and realized what he had done.

Quickly looking around he saw that nobody had noticed. Jasper had walked away so he waved his hand over the area on fire and the fire disappeared. He then lit the candles the mortal way.

After the food was gone everyone went home except for Jasper. Jasper said Ben should throw another party sometime.

That gave Ben an idea. Now he wants to have a pool party and this time he promises not to use magic on anything.

Rodeo Riot

I am a bull named Logan and ever since I was a calf I have lived on a farm in the Mortal Realm.

I haven't always been a familiar, but a couple of years ago my warlock Leon, decided that he wanted a familiar.

When he asked his parents for one they told him that it was already hard enough to care for all the farm animals and they weren't willing to add to the numbers.

During this time Leon watched the cattle a lot, and among the cattle was me, the farm bull.

Sometimes I would walk up to the fence and Leon would scratch me behind the ears.

As the days went by the relationship between us grew. Soon Leon started bringing me treats and eventually he got the idea that I could be his familiar.

After talking about it for a little while, Leon's parents decided that I could be sent to the Other Realm to be given the ability to talk and get trained to become a familiar.

As soon as I was ready, I was sent back to the farm to be Leon's familiar.

Leon is the type of warlock who uses magic without considering what could happen. Usually he ends up getting himself into trouble and will use magic to get out of it. In the end he usually manages to fix the magical messes that he creates.

This is about one of those times. I am going to tell you about the time that Leon and I went to a rodeo together.

One day Leon came to my pasture to talk to me. He asked me if I wanted to go to a rodeo.

Leon's parents are both witches and they had told him earlier that he could use his magic to go to a rodeo as long as he took me with him. I'm not sure they had really thought things through when they said this.

After I agreed to go with Leon, he told me that I could watch the rodeo from one of the bull pen's. I was okay with it because I thought that Leon would put me into an empty pen, and he did...sort of.

I was standing around in the pen when all of a sudden a saddle was being put onto my back. I realized that the people in charge of getting the bulls ready to be ridden thought that I was one of the bulls that was supposed to be ridden in the rodeo.

Luckily Leon noticed this and he quickly switched places with the person that he believed was in charge of the whole rodeo. As this person, Leon went to the pen I was in.

Before he could say or do anything to me, I asked him, "Why didn't you put me in the pen with the spare bulls?"

"There wasn't one," Leon replied.

"Well the pens for the bulls being ridden should have been full," I said. I was trying to figure out why there would be an empty pen when there weren't that many bull pen's to fill.

"They were full," Leon replied guiltily.

"So then where is the bull that is supposed to be in this pen?" I asked, wondering what Leon would do with a bull.

"It's right here," Leon replied reaching into his shirt pocket. He then pulled out a plastic bull.

"You turned it into a toy!" I exclaimed. I didn't even want to know how he had managed to do that when there were mortals around taking care of the bulls.

"It was the only thing I could think of!" Leon replied defensively.

"All right, first zap me out of here. Next return the bull that belongs here to its pen," I instructed.

"There's no time," Leon replied. "Look."

I looked and saw that there were suddenly a lot more mortals around. Most of the newcomers were bull riders getting ready to ride their bulls.

Thinking quickly I said, "Okay you are currently in the body of the guy in charge of this whole rodeo, right?"

"I think so," Leon replied sounding a bit unsure of himself.

I decided to take the chance that he was the man in charge and I said, "Grab a rope and use it to lead me out of here!"

"Okay, I'll try," Leon replied.

Leon led me to an empty, open space which was probably unfilled parking spaces. Here he used his magic to send the plastic bull back to its pen and turn it back into a live bull.

Before he could do anything else he was caught by a police officer.

"Where are you going with the bull?" the police officer asked Leon.

"I'm taking him home," Leon replied casually.

"You're not allowed to do that," stated the police officer sternly.

"Why not? I'm in charge of the rodeo aren't I?" bluffed Leon.

"Yeah, the set up. You aren't allowed to touch the bulls," the police officer argued.

As soon as the police officer said this, Leon used magic to switch bodies with him.

"Leon, you know if you keep switching places with people, eventually someone is going to figure out that you are a warlock," I warned.

"That doesn't matter right now, and if I do this right that shouldn't happen," Leon said as he magically froze the police officer—who was now looking like the rodeo set up man—in place.

"Now let's find someplace where we can be alone so I can fix this mess," said Leon.

It didn't take us long to reach some woodlands. Leon then zapped me into a bull picture on a shirt. Then he switched back to himself, switched the set up guy and the police officer back into their correct bodies, and he unfroze the police officer.

Next Leon zapped the two of us home, turned me back into a bull and put me back into my pasture.

I am never going to another rodeo as a bull with Leon. Instead we will have DWW turn me into a human. Leon could do it, but I'm not sure if that would be against the rules.

I know Leon breaks the rules of magic sometimes, but the ones that he breaks are the ones that almost every witch or warlock does at some point in time, and they don't get into big trouble for doing it.

Sometimes I complain about how often he gets into trouble using magic, but in the end I love being his familiar.

I know that with a warlock like him around, I will never be bored.

The Magic
of
Winning

The Magic of Winning

My name is Hunter and I was sentenced by DWW to spend fifty years as a gray wolf.

Before I was a wolf, I would change into any wild animal that I wanted. But that's not why I got into trouble.

I got in trouble for letting mortals find out that I could do this, and I would change into any animal that they requested.

I thought that it wasn't a problem as long as they didn't find out that I was a warlock. The mortals just thought I was a shape shifter, not a witch.

Well, DWW and the Witches Council didn't see it that way, and now I am a familiar.

Because I am a familiar, I have a witch that I am in charge of training. Her name is Lizzie.

"Hey, Hunter, I set up an obstacle

course in my backyard. Do you want to race me on it?" Lizzie asked as she ran towards me.

I was sitting by a dead tree with a large hole at the bottom that I turned into a den for myself.

"Are you planning on using magic?" I asked.

"No, this is a magic free race!"

"Well, then let's go!" I said as I ran towards Lizzie's house which was located in the middle of the woods. It was also not far from my tree den.

As I ran I thought about how in the past Lizzie would never have considered racing me without the use of her magic. It wasn't really that long ago when she decided not to use magic for competition anymore.

When I first started working with Lizzie, she was the most competitive witch that I had ever met. Normally she liked to compete just for the fun of it, but one day things changed.

This is the story of that day.

"Hunter, can I change you into a dog so that we can enter the local agility contest being held in the park?" Lizzie asked.

"No," I replied.

"Why not?" she asked sounding confused. This was the first time that I had ever refused to do something with her.

"The agility competition is going to be serious competition. It isn't a show that is being held just for the fun of it," I explained.

"So the show won't be fun?"

"No, the show will *be* fun but it isn't a show *for* fun," I explained.

"What's the difference?" she asked.

"The way you compete isn't right for a serious competition," I said.

"What are you talking about," she asked.

At this point, I was starting to confuse myself. I decided that instead of trying to explain things to Lizzie, I would make her see what I was talking about. So I said, "I'm sure you will find out soon."

"If you say so. Let's race to your den!" Lizzie suddenly decided as she ran off in the direction of my tree den. We were in her house at the moment.

"Okay," I replied.

I started running and I caught up to Lizzie very quickly, but as soon as she saw my tree den coming up she used magic to give herself the speed of a cheetah. Because of this she reached my den seconds before I did.

As soon as I got the chance I said, "Lizzie, there is a race coming up soon where you could compete against mortals in a serious competition."

"Really?" Lizzie asked interested.

"Yeah, why don't you sign up for it?" I asked hoping that she would say yes.

"All right, I will!"

When the day of the race came, Lizzie came to my house and told me that she was going to the race. I couldn't go with her because there was no woodland near where the race was being held.

She promised me that she would let me know how it went as soon as she returned. I already had an idea of how the race would go.

First the race would begin. Then as soon as enough mortals passed her she would try to use her magic for extra speed, but it won't work and she will lose the race. I didn't really want her to lose the race, but this was the best way for her to figure out what I was talking about earlier.

Later that day Lizzie ran up to me and exclaimed, "I won!"

"How?" I asked sounding a bit more surprised then I should have. "Your magic wouldn't have worked."

"It didn't, and how did you know that my magic wouldn't work?" she asked suspiciously.

"Magic can't be used to win serious competitions. In order to be able to use magic, the competition must be for fun only," I explained.

"So you were expecting me to lose?" Lizzie asked.

"Yes," I admitted. Then trying to get myself out of trouble and hoping to change the subject, I said, "But you won and now you know why I didn't want to do the agility contest."

"Actually, I still don't really understand that," she said thoughtfully.

"I didn't want to do it because you wouldn't have been able to use magic and then if I lost you would have been mad at me for it," I explained

"But maybe you could have won," Lizzie suggested. "You run really fast."

"Maybe," I said.

"So, do you want to enter the next agility contest and find out?" Lizzie asked.

"You want to do it even though you won't be able to use magic?" I asked her.

"Yeah, it turns out that winning without magic is pretty magical...at least in the way it feels," she said proudly.

"Does that mean you like winning the mortal way?"

"I guess so."

"Well then let's sign up for the next agility competition!" I said excitedly.

"Thanks Hunter!" Lizzie exclaimed.

Then she thought about something. "Hunter?" she asked.

"What?" I responded.

"If I can't use magic for the agility competition, then what would happen if I took you as a dog?"

"The spell would wear off and

I would be a wolf," I replied. When I realized what that meant, I said, "Wolves can't enter the competition."

"Then we can't do it," Lizzie said, sounding disappointed.

"I guess not," I agreed. I could tell that she was really disappointed.

"Well, what if someone else turned you into a dog," Lizzie suggested.

"It would be the same thing... unless." I suddenly had an idea.

"Unless what!" Lizzie exclaimed.

"Unless DWW performed the spell on me." I suggested.

"Do you think that she would?" Lizzie asked hopefully.

"It's possible, why don't we go now and ask her?"

Lizzie and I went to the Other Realm and asked DWW if I could be a dog for the agility competition. DWW allowed me to be a dog for the day of the agility competition only.

The day of the agility competition arrived and Lizzie and I won it.

Ever since then, anytime Lizzie competes with someone either in a serious competition or in a fun one, she chooses to do it without magic. That includes the times she knows she won't win, like now.

I will beat her easily on her own obstacle course.

Time's Up?

Prelude: Part Two

The following stories are examples of how a familiar's punishment can end by passing certain tests.

Each test is designed to see if the familiar learned from their earlier mistakes, and could therefore be trusted to follow the rules in the future.

Will they all pass?

Trisco

Trisco

My name is Trisco and I used to be a black squirrel. I was sentenced to one hundred and twenty-five years as one, but I was let go twenty-five years early.

You probably don't know exactly what happens when a familiar's punishment ends. You would think all that happens is that they get turned back into a witch or warlock, but it's not.

In order for you to understand what happens, I will tell you about what happened to me.

It was a Friday afternoon, and I was thinking about the fact that I still had twenty-five years to go until my sentencing was up when suddenly I found myself in the Other Realm. DWW had been the one who zapped me there.

"You are probably wondering why you are here," DWW said.

"Yes, I am," I replied.

"I have decided to end your punishment."

"Really? That's great because the neighbor's cat wants to kill me!"

"Why? What did you do this time?" DWW asked.

"Well, I sort of fell out of a tree and landed on it," I explained.

"That's your third time this month!" exclaimed DWW.

"I know, but it's better than last month! Last month I fell out of trees six times."

"You fall out of trees more than anybody else and you have been living in them for one hundred years!" DWW said.

I didn't say anything else because I could tell that she was trying her hardest not to laugh at me.

"Are you ready to prove yourself?" DWW asked, completely changing the subject.

"Yes, I am," I replied eagerly.

This is the next part of ending a familiar's sentence. The familiar must prove that they deserve to become a witch or warlock again.

"Okay, you got turned into a familiar because you used magic around mortals all the time where they could see you. Then you used illegal mind erasing spells to make them forget what they had seen. So here is what you are going to do," said DWW.

"You are going to be sent back into the Mortal Realm. A crowd of mortals who believe that you are a witch will be there. You will need to convince them that you aren't a witch without lying, using mind erase spells, any kind of deception spells, or any kind of magic to make them believe that you aren't a witch. You will be allowed to use any other kind of spells that you want," DWW explained.

"So, I can use magic where they can see it?" I asked.

"Yes, but only for this test. If you pass and become a warlock again permanently, you will still need to hide your powers from them," DWW cautioned.

"Okay, so when does the test start?" I asked, beginning to feel excited.

"How about I turn you back into a warlock now and you can spend the rest of today and tonight in the Other Realm to have some time getting used to being a warlock again. Tomorrow morning, come back here and I will send you to your test in the Mortal Realm," said DWW.

"Sounds fine with me," I agreed.

DWW then turned me back into a warlock, and I went to a friend's house to practice using my magic again.

The next day I went back to see DWW.

"Trisco are you ready to start your test?" DWW asked as soon as she saw me.

"Yes, I am," I said.

"Okay, do you remember the rules I

gave you?" DWW asked.

"Yes."

"Good, then the only other thing you should know is that I will be watching you the whole time. You are allowed to ask for hints when you need them, but only up to three, and you have five hours to complete your goal."

"What happens if I can't convince them in five hours? Does this mean that I will fail and become a squirrel again," I asked.

"No, what decides that is how you try to solve your problem," DWW explained. "It doesn't really matter how long it takes you to solve it."

"All right, then send me to the Mortal Realm."

DWW did, and I was immediately surrounded by mortals.

"Are you a witch?" one of them asked accusingly.

At first I wasn't sure how to answer this question since I wasn't allowed to lie to them. Then I thought about it and realized that I wasn't a witch, I was a warlock.

I was about to say no when I remembered something important. What I remembered was that a mixed group of witches and warlocks was simply addressed as witches so if I looked at it that way then I *was* a witch.

I then decided to use my first hint. I quickly froze the crowd and said, "DWW, I need a hint." I was then transported to the Other Realm.

"What kind of hint do you need?" she asked.

"How can I answer a direct question, like am I a witch, when I can't say yes because I am supposed to convince them otherwise, but if I say no then I would be lying because a group of witches and warlocks are known as witches?" I asked her.

"Well, then figure out a way to say no without lying," DWW suggested

"I can't, that isn't possible."

"It is, and that was your first hint."

She then zapped me back into
the Mortal Realm with me feeling more
confused than I had been before. I
realized that DWW wasn't likely to give
clear hints because I am supposed to be
figuring this out on my own.

Since the mortals were still frozen,
I decided to think about how to answer
the question. I decided that maybe I
didn't have to answer yes or no. DWW
may have been telling me to somehow lead
them off the subject.

I unfroze the mortals and hoped
that my plan would work, especially since
I was now down to four and a half hours.

"So are you a witch or not?" the
mortal asked again.

"Do you think that I am?" I asked.

"Well...a few people have claimed
that they have seen you do magic," the
mortal said.

"Yes, but do you believe them?" I
asked hoping she was a nonbeliever.

"No, but I am a news reporter and judging by what people have said about you—whether you are one or not—you are still hiding a secret," the mortal said accusingly.

"Okay, so you want to know my secret?" I asked hoping to keep the reporter distracted.

"Yes," answered the reporter.

"Then I will tell you," I said.

Luckily I had several secrets besides being a warlock so I could use one of them instead.

"So, what is your secret?" the mortal demanded.

"I am thirty years old and afraid of thunderstorms," I said.

This was actually true. I am probably one of the only warlocks to be afraid of thunder, even though witches and warlocks conjure up storms often when they are mad at someone. I am also only thirty in mortal years; in witch/ warlock years I am 300.

"That's your biggest secret?" she asked suspiciously.

I knew I was in trouble the minute she said biggest because it may have been a big secret for me, but my biggest was the one I couldn't tell so I couldn't say yes.

"It is one of them," I said.

"So, what's the one about you using magic?" she asked again.

Not seeing another way around it and considering I was now down to three and a half hours I said, "I can use magic, and I can do lots of magic tricks."

"So, you are more like a magician?" she asked.

"I can do any magician trick there is," I bragged hoping to convince her.

"Why don't you show me some of your tricks then," she demanded.

"Okay," I said.

Luckily I had pockets so I used them to zap up a deck of cards, a few coins, and a few scarves. I figured this would be enough to do the magic tricks.

I decided to perform the tricks I wanted the mortal way since I knew how.

After performing a few magic tricks I said, "Well, that's all I can do with what I have." It was true, I had done every magician trick I knew how to do.

"Do you always carry magic tricks in your pocket?" she asked.

"No, I only have them in there when I need them," I confessed.

"And, how do you know when you are going to need them?" she wondered.

"Well, if people ask me to do magic for them ahead of time I will carry them with me," I suggested. I was beginning to feel trapped again.

"So someone asked you to do magic

tricks for them?" she continued.

"Not recently," I confessed.

"Then why did you have the tricks in your pocket today?" she asked.

"Because you asked me to do them," I said knowing that I was in trouble.

"Did you know that you would be meeting me today and that you would be asked to do magic tricks?" she probed.

"No, but I did know I was going to be doing magic today," I said, beginning to feel worried again.

"How?" she asked.

"Does it matter?" I asked trying to distract her.

"Yes, because I know that you are still hiding something," she claimed.

"Okay, I am hiding something and you will never find out what it is," I said feeling like this conversation was not going so well.

"Why not?" she demanded.

"Because I am not going to tell you and that's all there is to it," I said. I knew I sounded like a bratty kid but I didn't care as long as it worked.

"For now maybe, but I will find out what you are hiding," she promised.

The reporter left and I realized that I had only two hours left. I had also managed to convince some of the mortals that I was only a magician.

I decided that the big part of my test probably was to convince the reporter I wasn't a witch above all the other mortals. I wondered if I didn't do this one thing would I fail? I decided to ask DWW for hint two.

I once again froze the mortals and said, "I need hint two." Immediately I was zapped into the Other Realm.

"What do you want to know this time?" DWW asked.

"How do I convince the reporter that I am not a witch," I asked her.

"Reporters follow the biggest story," suggested DWW.

"So, I have to lead her to a story that is bigger than the possibility of me being a warlock?" I asked.

"Sorry, I can't give you any more hints unless you want to use up your third one," DWW explained.

"I don't want to use up my third unless I really need it. You can send me back now," I requested.

She once again zapped me into the Mortal Realm, but before I unfroze the mortals, I decided to use a spell.

The spell was to make a UFO make a stop above the mortals if the reporter came back to find out my secret. I then unfroze the mortals.

For the next hour I did fake magic tricks for the mortals who asked.

Then the reporter came back, and asked "Does your *real* biggest secret involve magic?"

Before I had time to answer, my spell arrived. All the mortals around stopped to watch it and they followed behind it as it flew above their heads moving further away from them as it appeared to land.

Then it slowly rose back up, still moving away from the mortals with them chasing after it. As soon as it was completely out of sight, the mortals had been out of my sight for at least fifteen minutes.

I was now down to forty-five minutes till my test was over. For the next fifteen minutes I waited, but no mortals reappeared. I began to think all of them, including the reporter, had forgotten all about me, so I decided to spend my last half hour doing whatever I felt like.

At the end of the half hour, I was zapped back into the Other Realm.

"Your test is now over," DWW said.

"So, did I pass?" I asked.

"Yes, although you only managed to convince a few mortals. I knew you wouldn't be able to convince them all," DWW explained.

"You did?" I asked.

"Yes, the test was to show that not only can you hide magic from the average mortal, you can keep your secret even when a reporter is directly questioning you. Some mortals will believe you are a witch whether or not you use magic, and you will never be able to convince them all that you aren't," DWW explained.

"Now that I know you will be able to keep your secret, I can tell you that your time is up. You are now a full-time warlock and can live wherever you want. But I suggest that now that you are a warlock again, you stay out of trees," she added with a laugh.

"Yeah, and if I ever do end up being a familiar again, can I be something that doesn't live in them?"

"If it does happen again, I will consider it, but you better try your hardest to behave," DWW cautioned.

"I will," I promised.

"Then go," commanded DWW.

I left and went back to the Mortal Realm where I got a new house, and a familiar of my own. I got a German Shepherd puppy who was born a familiar and I named him Magic.

So that's how familiars usually end their sentences.

First they are turned back into a witch or warlock, and then they have to do something to prove they deserve to be one. And after that they either become a witch or warlock permanently or they become a familiar once again.

I know I really will try my hardest to behave so that I never have to be a familiar again.

Jake

Jake

"You are going to be sent to the Mortal Realm, where you will meet some mortals. All of them will know that you are a warlock, and will want to get into the Other Realm. All you have to do is last two days without letting them in," DWW said.

"That's it?" I asked.

"Yes," DWW replied.

"Okay, send me to the Mortal Realm." I was ready for my test.

"I will, tomorrow," DWW told me.

"Why tomorrow?" I asked.

"Tonight you are going to get used to being human again which may take a while," DWW explained.

"All right, I'll see you tomorrow then," I said, getting ready to zap myself somewhere else.

Before I could go DWW stopped me. "Jake," she said.

"What?" I asked.

"You have to stay in the Other Realm until your test."

"Okay," I agreed.

The next day I went to see DWW to start my test.

"Are you ready?" DWW asked me as soon as I arrived.

"Yes, I'm ready," I replied confidently. I was sure that I would pass my test.

"Do you remember your rules?" DWW questioned.

"I have to live in the Mortal Realm for the next two days and not let any mortals into the Other Realm, right?" I asked. This would be easy.

"That and you also have to avoid breaking any other rules," she added.

"I didn't plan on breaking any more," I promised.

"Your test will begin as soon as you arrive in the Mortal Realm," said DWW.

"Will I be sending myself there?"

"No, I will be sending you. If you sent yourself, how would you know where your test is at?" DWW asked.

"I guess I wouldn't, but I'm sure that I could," I said.

"Maybe. Well, good luck Jake," DWW said.

The next thing I knew I was in the Mortal Realm. I saw two mortals watching me. There was one guy and one girl.

"Hi, Jake," the guy said.

"Uh, hi," I replied, not recognizing either of them but figuring that they were the mortals that DWW had mentioned yesterday.

"How do you know me?" I asked.

"DWW told us that you were coming," the girl said.

"How? She wouldn't tell mortals that a warlock was coming," I said.

"So, are you sure we are mortals?" she asked.

"No, but you must be otherwise how could this be my test. I am supposed to avoid letting mortals into the Other Realm," I explained.

"Maybe your test hasn't arrived yet," she suggested.

"How would I know if you were mortals or witches?" I asked her.

"Well, witches have magical abilties," she offered.

"Okay, so can you use magic?" I asked suspiciously.

"Sure I can. What do you want me to do?" she asked.

"How about you conjure me up a cat?" I suggested.

"Okay," she agreed readily as she pointed at the ground.

Instantly a shorthaired black and white female cat appeared.

"So you are a witch," I said.

"To some people," she said.

"Can you do magic as well?" I asked the guy.

"Yes, do you want me to conjure up a cat as well?" he asked.

"Sure, but conjure up one that will get along with the other cat," I requested.

"I can do that," he replied.

He pointed and a male shorthaired gray tabby cat appeared.

"If both of you can do magic, then where are the mortals I am supposed to meet," I asked them.

"I don't know," the guy said.

"I don't know either," the girl replied. "Since you now know what we are, would you zap us into the Other Realm?"

"I guess I could," I replied.

I started to point at them, but before I did I thought about something. Some mortals can use magic. They are known as wizards, sorcerers, and sorceresses.

Wizards use wands so I knew that they weren't that, but I also decided that there was no way they could be witches. If they were, they could use their own powers to get into the Other Realm.

"Why don't you use your own magic?" I asked.

"We can't," the guy said.

"Why not?" I asked beginning to grow suspicious.

"We just can't," the girl said. "We'll see you tomorrow."

After that the two of them left using magic to transport themselves somewhere.

I was now sure that they were mortals, and there was no way I was letting them into the Other Realm.

The next day, I was walking by a park when all of a sudden my "test" popped up in front of me.

"Hi, again," the girl said.

"Hi," I replied. "I know that the two of you are mortals. What I don't know is why DWW told you that I was coming."

"Since you know, I guess I should explain," she said.

"You should," I agreed.

"Well, I was a witch once, and my friend was a warlock," she explained.

"Why aren't you still witches?" I asked curiously.

"That's easy. You know how the Head of the Witches Council gives you a choice between spending your sentence as a mortal or a witch's familiar?" she asked.

"Of course, DWW gave me that option." Obviously you know what I chose.

"We got our punishments for the same thing that you did, but we failed our test to get our powers back. Because of this we were sentenced to live in the Mortal Realm without our witchcraft forever," she explained.

"You both let mortals in the Other Realm during your test?" I asked her.

"Yes," she confessed.

"You should have at least waited until you weren't being watched by DWW," I suggested.

Right after I said that there was a flash of light and I found myself in the Other Realm facing DWW.

"Jake, are you implying that if I wasn't watching you, that you would let mortals into the Other Realm?" DWW asked me sternly.

"No, of course not," I replied. "I know that even if you weren't watching me I would get caught." I hoped that I had said enough to get myself out of trouble.

"All right, you can get back to your test, but be careful," she warned me.

Back in the Mortal Realm I knew that my test would be over in a few hours so I decided to talk to the mortals about the different types of magic.

I found out that once the two of them learned about the two different types of magic that mortals could use they decided to try sorcery.

I thought that it would be hard to learn since magic doesn't come easily to most mortals, but since they were witches once it was actually easy for them to learn it.

As soon as my test was over, DWW immediately brought me into the Other Realm.

"So did I pass?" I asked.

"You did," DWW replied.

"So do I get to remain a warlock?" I asked her.

"As long as you follow the rules," DWW warned.

"I will," I promised.

"Okay, then go do whatever you want," said DWW.

"Thanks," I said happily.

After that I returned to the Mortal Realm to live—happy to be a warlock once again.

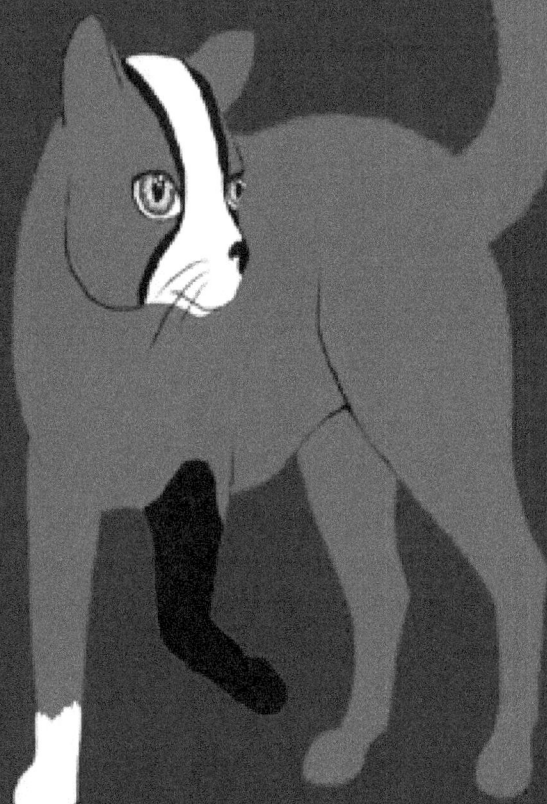

Plarklay

I was once a warlock, but now I am a cat...permanently. Recently I took my test to become a warlock again and failed.

I'm not going to tell you about my test because it was very similar to Jake's, whose test you already read about, with the exception that he passed and I failed. I also became a familiar the same way he did. Like Jake I let a mortal into the Other Realm.

Do you know what happens when a familiar fails their test? Nothing. They return to their familiar forms, and this is how they remain for the rest of their lives. The tests can't be retaken.

Would I want to retake my test if I could? Actually...no, I think I prefer being a cat now. This happens sometimes. Familiars can choose to remain the animal that they currently are rather than taking a test when their punishments are up. As you might know, Trillman, who recently became DWW's familiar for the second time, chose this path.

So, you might wonder what my plans are now. Well, I am going to return to the Mortal Realm where I have been living as a traveler cat. Specifically I have been living in woods because I really like wooded areas, except for in the winter. In the winter I usually find a warm barn to stay in.

What is a traveler cat? Being a traveler cat is almost exactly the same as being a stray, except that I live this way by choice. I suppose I would be willing to become someone's familiar, and live with them, if the right magic user came along, but for now that's not what I will be doing.

By the way, because I live in your Realm, maybe I should describe myself to you in case you are interested.

My name is Plarklay, and like my name, I am a little unusual. I mean my *looks* are unusual. As for being a cat, I think I am the average Mortal Realm cat, aside from my past and being able to talk.

You should also recall that I mentioned my markings are unusual as well.

Maybe I should have just said my personality is average for a cat. Yeah, I think that works better.

Anyway, I am a mostly brown cat with a white tail tip and a thick black line directly under that. I have a big white blaze that covers most of my face except for on the right side. I also have two black lines on my face by my eyes, and my eyes are green.

There is a thick black line just above my right front leg and the paw is white. My left front leg is completely black and the paw is white. My eyes are green.

So that's me. Maybe you will see me again some day.

Hunter

You probably remember me as Hunter, the wolf familiar. I had a witch called Lizzie who was very competitive.

I am not her familiar anymore.

Why not? Because today my sentence ends; or at least it will as long as I pass my test.

Currently I am in the Other Realm waiting for another familiar's test to end. I expect to wait for about half an hour until DWW calls me to come see her.

I have no idea what my test is going to be. It's different for each familiar.

"Hunter are you ready for your test?" DWW asks me as she walks into the room.

"I think so," I reply. I'm not really sure what to expect.

"Your test is going to be short and it shouldn't be very hard," DWW tells me.

"What do I have to do?" I ask.

"You will have to change into different living things to reach a specific goal," DWW replies.

"Wait, I am supposed to change into things?" I ask confused. "But that's how I got into trouble in the first place."

"I know, but this is different. You will be in a place with mortals, but you won't be allowed to let any of them see you," DWW says.

"They can't see me change?" I ask her, thinking that this is what she is talking about.

"They can't see you at all no matter what you are," DWW specifies.

"How am I supposed to do that?" I ask confused. That can't be possible to do, can it?

"If I told you, then this wouldn't be much of a test," DWW replies, not willing to give me any hints.

"Okay, so what goal do I have to reach?" I ask. I remembered DWW mentioned something about one earlier.

"The goal will be a potted plant. It will be sitting on the desk of a mortal. All you will have to do is reach it, without being seen, duplicate the plant and the pot, then transport the original plant back to me," DWW explains.

"That part doesn't sound too hard. What's the catch?" I ask, knowing that there's no way it could be that simple.

"The mortal will be in the room," DWW replies.

"That would make it harder," I say.

"Do you want to begin your test now?" DWW asks me.

"Don't familiars usually get a day to get used to being human again?" I ask.

"Usually, but there's no need for this. You will be changing into other living things. You won't be taking this test as a human," DWW explains.

"Okay, so can I be any living thing that I want?" I ask getting an idea of an animal that would be perfect for the situation I was going to be in.

"Only if it exists in the Mortal Realm. You won't be allowed to become anything that is exclusive to the Other Realm," DWW replies looking at me as if she can tell exactly what I am thinking. "Is there anything else that you want to know?" she asks me.

"No, I believe that I know everything that I need to for my test at this point," I reply.

"So, do you want to begin now?" DWW asks, sounding as if she really wants to get started on my test.

"Sure," I reply confidently. I am sure I can pass this test.

"All right. You will be zapped outside of a two floor building with seven offices on each floor. All you need to do is get to room three on the second floor," DWW instructs me.

"Okay, you can zap me there now," I say. I am eager to get started.

A few seconds later I find myself exactly where DWW said that I would. I scan the yard surrounding the building and see no mortals.

Next I look for a way in that I
can use without being seen. I don't see
anything on the side of the building where
I am standing so I decide to go around
and check in front.

Up until the walkway to the
building there is a lot of tall grass so I
turn myself into a spider. I stop when I
reach the end of the grass.

I am about to run up to the front
door to see if there were any cracks in it
that I can use to enter the building when
I feel heavy vibrations. Like most bugs, I
feel vibrations instead of hearing sounds.

It isn't long before I see a human
with a guide dog in training, a young
German Shepherd, approaching. As soon
as the dog is directly in front of me, I turn
myself into a flea and jump into its fur.

In order to make sure I would stay
on, I bite the dog and hold on. I am lucky
it appears to have learned to focus on it's
task rather than other things because
most other dogs would have tried to
bite and scratch me off of them at that
moment.

Now I need to decide what to do once I am inside the building.

It turns out that I don't need to worry about this because I feel the dog head upstairs and turn into the room where I need to be. As a flea I feel the dog stop and feel vibrations that I instinctively know come from two people talking.

Only a moment passes before I feel someone approaching the dog. I guess that it is the person who owns the plant that I need to get to. I begin to consider how I would reach the plant and decide I need to use the mortal to get to it.

I know that I need to become something that is invisible to people, but what? As a flea I am small but I could still get spotted.

Thinking about it, I realize that DWW had specified that I could only turn into living things from the Mortal Realm, but that doesn't mean I have to turn myself into an animal.

Just in time I turn myself into a germ and attached myself to the right person as soon as I feel their hand touch the dog. Now all I need to do is get to the potted plant.

I think about this for a while. How can I get the person that I am on to touch the plant?

Once again the dog becomes the answer to my problem. It's a good thing that dogs in training make mistakes occasionally.

The dog's owner lets the young dog off of its harness. The dog, thinking that it's job is over now that the harness is off, gets excited. In it's excitement it accidentally knocks the plant off of the desk. After this happens, the dog's owner reharnesses the dog and takes it out of the room to refocus. The plant's owner then goes to pick up the plant.

As soon as the hand I am on touches the plant, I slide off the hand and onto the plant. I begin feeling really excited now. I reached my goal and now all I have to do is duplicate the plant and get it to DWW. The only problem is that I can't do it with the mortal still in the room.

I decide to wait until the mortal went home for the day. While I am waiting, I turn myself into a flea again in order to feel the vibrations that would tell me as soon as the room was empty.

Eventually the lights go out. The vibrations of the mortal stop. I wait. They don't seem to be coming back.

After waiting a few minutes longer I am sure that I am alone in the room, but I remain a flea rather than turn human just in case. If someone did happen to come into the room I could still easily hide from them as a flea.

As a flea, I duplicate the plant, set it next to the original then magically transport myself and the original plant back to DWW.

As soon as I arrive in the Other Realm, DWW tells me that I have passed my test, and then she asks me, "Did you like your test?"

That's a strange question, I think to myself. Out loud I say, "Yes, I actually did." I meant it too.

"So do you like the challenge of hiding your magic or using it openly in front of mortals better?" DWW asks.

Another strange question, I think. To DWW I reply, "I really like the challenge of changing into things and trying to hide from mortals best."

"Does this mean that you will use your abilities secretly from now on?" DWW asks.

"Yes, I will," I answer truthfully.

"Good, you are now officially a warlock again. You can go now," she says.

"All right, thanks," I say as I zap myself out of the Other Realm.

As I arrive in the Mortal Realm, I decide to enter my first mortal competition as a human.

Depending on the competition I enter, maybe I will see Lizzie there and we can compete for real, not just for fun.

Mortal Realm Witch

Realms Unite?

By
Jennifer Priester

Book Three Available Now!

DWW wants to unite the Other Realm and the Mortal Realm. In Book Three, *Mortal Realm Witch: Realms Unite?,* this is exactly what DWW will be trying to do.

To help her accomplish her goals many former characters will return including: Travis, Alaska, Ally, Air Raid, Taron, Turtle, Sam, Star, Max, and more.

You will also get to meet some new characters including: a black panther familiar, two young animal psychics and their pets, and others.

Along the way you will learn about Head Journals, more about DWW, and discover some new and surprising facts about the events leading up to her becoming the Head of the Witches Council.

You will also get to learn new things about the former Head, Trom, such as the things he did during his rule as the

Head of the Witches Council, and a big secret that very few people know about him.

You will also get to meet and learn about some of the creatures that live in the Other Realm. Some of the creatures you will meet are: the Mystical Chi, the Starlight Rabbit, and the Mysterious Mastiff.

Everyone you meet, and everything you learn in this book will lead you to one big event...the unification of the Realms. But are witches and mortals as ready for this as DWW believes them to be?

To find out the answer read *Mortal Realm Witch: Realms Unite* available now!

To find out more about the Mortal Realm Witch series, other books in progress, and to enjoy some activities, please visit our website at: **www.mortalrealmwitch.com.**

Mortal Realm Witch:

Learning About Magic

By
Jennifer Priester

Mortal Realm Witch:

The Magic Continues

By
Jennifer Priester

Books One & Two Available Now!

In Book One, *Mortal Realm Witch: Learning About Magic*, you will meet DWW back when she was a young witch just discovering her magical powers.

In this book you will learn what DWW's name stands for and what it means. You will also learn what events took place leading up to DWW's becoming the Head of the Witches Council, and enjoy DWW's other earlier adventures as she learns how to use her newly discovered powers and learns all about witches.

Throughout the stories you will not only learn about DWW, but discover how Trillman and Trom saw her as they share their stories about what it was like to train her in magic.

You will meet Ally, a young witch who is searching for the right familiar.

When Ally finds a dragon, called Air Raid, she decides that she wants him to be her familiar, but she is told that dragons don't make good familiars.

Now Ally will have to prove that dragons can be good familiars, but this won't be easy. In this story you will also learn about some of the rules about witches, and how DWW impacted change in the rules.

In Book Two, *Mortal Realm Witch: The Magic Continues,* you learn more about DWW's adventures as her new life in the Other Realm begins, bringing with it more and often bigger challenges.

You will meet Turtle, a young witch, whose adventures will help continue the main story. DWW will be there to help Turtle learn about her powers and teach you even more about magic.

Then a big threat to all witches will be discovered! Everything will lead up to one big event--possibly the biggest event in all witch/mortal history!

To find out more about the Mortal Realm Witch Series, visit our website at: **www.mortalrealmwitch.com**.

About the Author

About the Author

Jennifer Priester is an author and an artist. She loves animals and has a Chihuahua whose name is Taco, a Mini-Rex rabbit named Kojikaki, and a really old goldfish whose name is Pumpkin. She has adopted most of her animals from rescue centers.

She also enjoys taking her dog for bike rides, spending time outdoors, taking photos of animals, horseback riding, reading, listening to music, watching TV and movies, and playing video games.

Jennifer has written over 200 stories in the areas of animals, the relationships between humans and animals, magic, superheroes and more.

To learn more about the author, visit **www.jenniferpriester.com** and to learn more about the series visit **www.mortalrealmwitch.com.**

You can also find the author on Facebook, Goodreads, and many other places as well. Find the links to all these places on her website.